Nani's
Holiday

Also by Lisa Bruce

Jazeera's Journey
Jazeera in the Sun
Oh Omar!

Banana Books

Sister of the Bride

Lisa Bruce

Nani's Holiday

Illustrated by Paul Howard

mammoth

For Mum and Dad

First published in Great Britain 1994
by Methuen Children's Books Ltd
Published 1995 by Mammoth
an imprint of Reed International Books Limted
Michelin House, 81 Fulham Road, London SW3 6RB

Reprinted 1997, 1998

Text copyright © 1994 Lisa Bruce
Illustrations copyright © 1994 Paul Howard

The right of Lisa Bruce to be identified as
author of this work has been asserted by her in accordance
with the Copyright, Designs and Patents Act 1988

ISBN 0 7497 2331 9

A CIP catalogue record for this title
is available from the British Library

Printed and bound in Great Britain
by Cox & Wyman Ltd, Reading, Berkshire

Contents

1. Nani's Here

No one had told Jazeera that Nani was coming, so it had been a complete surprise to her when she had spied the little white-robed figure struggling through the Arrivals gate. Since moving to England, Jazeera had missed her Nani more than anyone else. As soon as she had seen her, Jazeera had leapt over the barrier and rushed to her grandmother like a young tornado.

Jazeera's fingers glided over the soft leather spine of the new book. The empty pages fanned delicately in her hands, sending leathery wafts of air up to her nostrils. The book was so solid, so

important-looking. It was the best present that Jazeera had ever had. Her grandmother had given it to her. Happily, she leant forward and gave the brown face beside her a kiss.

'Thank you, Nani,' Jazeera said softly. 'A diary, just like yours. It's perfect.'

Nani watched Jazeera scribbling away on the first page and smiled. She knew her little granddaughter very well.

Now, with the gifts all distributed, Jazeera sat on the sofa beside her grandmother. It was a bumpy experience because her little brother Omar, on the other side of Nani, was bouncing up and down, continuously.

'Stop jumping, Omar,' scolded his mother. 'Poor Nani will get seasick!'

'It's all right,' smiled Nani. 'He's just excited, that's all.'

A cry from the bedroom caught their mother's attention and she left the room. She returned carrying a small bundle.

'Here she is!' Jazeera's mother smiled, walking towards the sofa. 'Grandchild number four. You must sit still, Omar, Nani is going to hold Azra.'

Their mother placed the little bundle in Nani's outstretched arms and for a while Omar did sit still. He liked his baby sister, when she wasn't crying, that was.

'Isn't she beautiful,' Nani said. 'She's got Mohammed's smile, hasn't she?'

Everyone looked at Jazeera's father to see whether this was the case, murmuring their agreement. Then the baby let out a shrill wail.

'Omar!' everybody cried.

Omar wanted to play with his little sister. He had grabbed Azra's foot and was twisting it uncomfortably.

'I'm playing the counting game,' he explained. 'On her toes, like Jaz does.'

'Yes,' said Nani, removing the tiny foot carefully from his grasp. 'But, you have to be gentle with her. She is only little.'

Omar's eyes shone with sudden understanding.

'Nani, do you know, Azra was so little that she was born in a fish tank.'

'No, she wasn't, Omar,' said Jazeera. 'It was an incubator, not a fish tank.'

Omar looked aggrieved at being corrected and Azra set up a plaintive cry of hunger. Jazeera's mother bent down and scooped the baby up in her arms.

'I'll feed her, then one of you two can come and help me change her nappy.'

'Me, me, I'll do it,' said Omar happily.

'I'll be the cream holder for you. I'm good at doing that,' he told Nani, importantly.

As Omar trotted off after their mother, Jazeera slipped her hand into Nani's, gripping it tightly. Jazeera couldn't really believe what was happening. It was so unexpected, so overwhelmingly impossible that she thought Nani might vanish if she let her out of her sight.

Nani smiled down at her favourite granddaughter and quickly changed the expression on her face to one of concern.

'Why, Jazeera, whatever is the matter?' she exclaimed.

Jazeera was silent.

'You're crying,' Nani said, wiping a silvery tear from Jazeera's moist cheek. 'What's wrong?'

Jazeera sniffed, then gulped.

'I'm . . . I'm happy,' Jazeera said in a strangled voice. 'I'm so glad you're here, Nani.'

'So am I,' Nani whispered.

Nani put her arm around Jazeera and held her very tight.

Later that day Nani sat at the table. She adjusted her glasses and began to write to her old friend, Mrs Khan.

12 July

Dear Kurshid,
Just a note to let you know that we have all arrived safely. I know how much you worry about me. The journey on the aeroplane was very long and tiring but the flight attendants made sure that I was comfortable.

Ahh, how nice it is to be here with the family! The children have grown so much in the last year and baby Azra is a darling, you would love her. How nice it is to be a grandmother again.

It was a delight to see Jazeera at the airport. Her face was a picture! She had no idea that I was on the flight and she was absolutely over the moon to see me. Jazeera has hugged me and squeezed me to death since then. In fact the only time that she let go of my hand was to open the little diary that I gave her. She was thrilled to get it and has promised to write in it every day.

Salma was delighted with the saree that you sent for her. The colour suits her perfectly. She says that she is going to take it on her honeymoon. They are going to Italy. Salma is looking very grown up now. I can hardly believe that it is ten years since I last saw her, she was just a young girl like Jazeera and now she is getting married.

How are you enjoying your retirement? Life must be quiet for you without all those naughty schoolchildren around you all day. And how is Shebu? I am surprised at how attached I have grown to the naughty little dog. I hope that she is not chewing up your furniture. It was very kind of you to look after her while we are away.

Mohammed took us all out for a meal to his restaurant. It is called 'A Taste of

India' and business must be good because all the tables were full. We had a special table reserved for us. I did feel important. After we had eaten, Mohammed showed us around the kitchens and to the upstairs room which is hired out for parties. Salma's mendhi ceremony will be held there this Friday.

But before the wedding, there is another important ceremony that I am told I must attend . . .

Yours,

Nani

2. A Shock for Jazeera

Butterflies tumbled inside her stomach as Jazeera sat stiffly on the stage. Without looking at the sea of faces in the audience, in case she lost her concentration, Jazeera reached forward and stroked the silken piano keys. At once, notes tumbled out and chased away her nerves. Jazeera began to play.

This was the end of term gathering, when prizes were handed out and speeches made. Jazeera, who had won the Outstanding Musician Award, had been asked to give a recital. Under her lithe fingers the music came alive and Jazeera felt it flow out of her, swelling

until it filled the whole of the school hall.

Jazeera had been so proud when she had been asked to play at the concert. Now, she especially wanted to play well for her Nani, the Nani who had first taught her scales and to love the piano as she did. She stopped as the final note echoed into silence. Then there was a moment of visible tension followed by a roar of applause.

Grinning from plait to plait, Jazeera turned to face the audience, and with a deep bow she acknowledged their praise. Only now could she permit herself to look at the rows of faces. At the front, her family beamed proudly. Nani raised her clapping hands and Jazeera saw a pearly tear slide down her cheek.

Nani liked it.

Jazeera breathed a gasp of relief as she walked up to shake hands with Mrs Levin, the headmistress, and to collect her book token. Clutching the slim white envelope in her clammy palms, Jazeera returned to her seat with the rest of her class.

'Well done,' whispered Moni.

Amy squeezed her arm. 'Yeah, Jaz, you were brill.'

Jazeera grinned at her two friends, then smiled across the hall at Nani who was still clapping.

'Jazeera, could you come here for a minute, please,' Mrs Levin called from the door of her office. 'Is that your family?' she asked. 'Please ask them to join us, Jazeera.'

Jazeera led her family into the head's office and saw a well-dressed woman, smelling of expensive perfume, waiting on one of the comfortable chairs. From the smile on her face Jazeera knew that she wasn't in trouble.

'Now,' said the head in her most headmistressly voice, 'I have just had some very exciting news. This is Miss McCarthy from the Highthorn

Academy. She heard Jazeera play and she was very impressed.'

'More than that, Mrs Levin,' smiled Miss McCarthy. 'I think that we can consider Jazeera for a place at our school.'

She beamed broadly in Jazeera's direction.

Several sets of brown eyes stared blankly at her, not really understanding what she meant. Mrs Levin began to explain.

'I'm sure you are aware that when our pupils leave here most of them transfer to the county comprehensive.'

Jazeera's parents nodded.

'Well,' continued Mrs Levin, 'I have taken the liberty of also putting Jazeera's name down for a specialist music school. Highthorn only takes top-quality musicians, so the fact that they are prepared to consider Jazeera is quite an achievement for her.'

Jazeera's father shook his head doubtfully.

'I've never heard of this school,' he admitted.

'It is about forty miles away, Jazeera would have to stay during the week,' the smart woman explained.

'Oh, I'm sorry, we can't afford anything like that.'

'Of course not,' put in Mrs Levin soothingly. 'This is for a scholarship place. If Jazeera is successful, her board and fees will be paid for.'

She smiled down at Jazeera.

'This is a most marvellous opportunity for the whole school, not just Jazeera. I'm sure you must be delighted.'

'No I'm not,' snapped Jazeera suddenly. 'I don't want to go.' She spun on her heel and ran out of the crowded office, dangerously close to crying in public.

Glancing out of the big windows, Nani saw Jazeera running across the playground towards an old garden shed.

Nani slipped out of a side door and quietly followed her. There, in a dip in the ground behind the shed surrounded by a forest of nettles, Jazeera sat clutching her knees, crying softly. Nani gathered up the skirts of her saree and slithered down into the hollow next to her. Jazeera didn't look up.

'Well, I must say, you don't look like a girl who's just made a successful debut in front of hundreds of admiring parents. I thought that you might have been out greeting your fans, signing autographs, things like that.'

Jazeera didn't speak.

Nani didn't appear to notice, she continued as though she were having a pleasant chat with a neighbour.

'By the way, did I write to you about Anil? I'm sure that I meant to. Mrs Khan has a new cook and Anil is her son. Come to think of it, he must be about the same age as you. He's ever such a bright boy, really good at his studies. I met him once and he told me that he wanted to

be a doctor. He had such wonderful hopes. It's a pity about what has happened to him.'

Despite herself Jazeera couldn't help listening to Nani's tale. She lifted her head a fraction and asked, 'Why, what did happen?'

'Poor old Anil, his village is very close to the river and he was devastated when the rains came, last year. The monsoon was heavier than usual. I remember how much it rained at the time but I had no idea what was happening in the low-lying areas.

'The river grew swollen and bloated. It was gorged with water until finally it could take no more. The banks burst and the muddy water gushed into the fields beside it. Unfortunately, Anil's village was next to the fields and within minutes they were flooded out. Most people climbed to safety on the roofs of their houses but one little girl got swept away from her mother in the strong swirling current.

'There was a man who could see that she was being carried along to the schoolhouse. It was only a rough building with mud walls and a thatched roof, not very strong at all. The water was damaging the walls of the schoolhouse far worse than other buildings because it was nearest to the river bank.

'The man realised what was going to happen, he could see the schoolhouse quivering and shaking and the little girl moving rapidly into the danger area. At once, he plunged into the swelling waters and battled his way down to the broken building. Just in time, he caught the little girl's arm and hauled her aside. The walls gave way and the roof collapsed, missing her by inches.'

By now Jazeera was sitting in rapt attention. Hearing the story of such a heroic man pushed her own troubles to the back of her mind.

'That was brave of him,' she said.

'Yes,' nodded Nani, sadly. 'Very brave

and courageous because although the little girl was saved, one of the beams fell on the man. It knocked him unconscious and he drowned.'

'No!' Jazeera gasped. 'But, Nani, what about Anil? What happened to him?'

Nani gently sighed. 'That man was Anil's father.'

The weight of Nani's words pressed Jazeera's heart into her stomach.

'So you see, not only did Anil lose his school but worse, he lost his father.'

'What has happened to him, Nani?'

'He's helping his mother now, in the houses where she works, running errands, doing odd jobs . . .'

'Doesn't he go to school any more?' Jazeera asked, concerned.

'How can he?' Nani sighed. 'The schoolhouse was washed away and, with his father gone, who will pay for his school fees? The one chance that Anil had to do something in his life has been taken away from him.'

Jazeera swallowed and stared

thoughtfully down at her navy-blue sandals. Silence settled between them until Jazeera said quietly, 'Nani, do you think that I should go to Highthorn?'

Nani did not answer. She plucked a blade of grass from the ground and folded it around her fingers.

'You would be doing the wrong thing if you went there determined to be unhappy.'

'But that's just it. How can I be happy there, when Amy and Moni and all the others from the class will be going to the county comp?'

'Amy and Moni are very fortunate to be able to go to the county comprehensive,' Nani said. 'Just think what someone like Anil would give to have that opportunity.'

Jazeera looked up and gazed into Nani's deep brown eyes.

'And I'm even luckier to have the chance to go to Highthorn, I suppose.

Nani's eyes twinkled behind her thin, gold-rimmed glasses. She sighed and pulled herself up.

'Come on, Jazeera, I guess that we'd better be getting back before they send search parties out for us.'

3. Wedding Surprise

Dear Diary,

You are a wonderful present. Nani was so clever to think of giving you to me. I am going to write in you every day, just like Nani does in her diary. Then, when I'm old, I'll be able to look back and see what happened to me.

It is so exciting having Nani here. Uncle Salim and Aunty Naseema will have to go back to India after Salma Apa's wedding, but Nani is going to stay for a long holiday.

Today Nani came with me to my piano lesson. She pushed Azra in the pram. She says that she wished that she

28

had one when Mummy was a baby.

Nani cuddled Azra while I had my lesson. I did all my pieces perfectly because I knew that Nani was listening. Afterwards Susan, my teacher, had a long chat with Nani. They really liked each other.

Mummy was cross with Omar today. She and Aunty Rehanna were so busy getting ready for the wedding that they didn't see Omar messing around by the bag of dates. They are a present for Kabir's parents and Omar knocked them all over the floor! It took Mummy and Aunty ages to pick them all up. Omar has been sent to his room.

Mummy has ironed my new suit and everything has been set out ready for the wedding tomorrow. Nani has said that she will do my hair in a French plait. Mummy can't do those.

Jazeera stared in wonder at her cousin's sequinned saree as it glittered in the strong light of the video camera. A cameraman scurried around Salma as she posed for the video surrounded by various members of her family. The little living room was full to bursting point with relatives from all over the country.

When she was called, Jazeera took her place proudly beside Salma Apa and smiled at the camera. Jazeera thought that her cousin looked stunning, like a film star, swathed in deep red and covered in gold jewellery.

Salma stood serenely, with eyes lowered, while her family each appeared beside her on the video.

'Nearly finished now,' said the cameraman.

'Wait a minute,' cried Jazeera. She realised that one very important person was missing. 'Nani's not here.'

Jazeera ran into the kitchen where she found her grandmother busy washing up.

'Come on, Nani,' laughed Jazeera, tugging at Nani's white saree. 'It's your

31

turn to be on the video.'

'Oh, but I'm all wet.'

Nani dried her hands and followed Jazeera into the crowded living room. People stood aside letting Nani through to stand beside her eldest granddaughter.

'Smile, please,' called the cameraman.

Nani winked at Jazeera and gave her broadest beam to the camera.

At last everyone was ready and the wedding party set off for the Civic Hall. Jazeera sat beside Nani in the car, She felt very grown up in her new purple and gold *salwar kameeze*. Salma Apa had even bought her some matching bangles. Jazeera could hardly keep still in the car, she was so excited.

Jazeera glanced through the back window to the car behind. There, behind the fluttering red ribbons, sat Salma Apa.

'Salma Apa looks a bit sad,' Jazeera said thoughtfully.

'Of course she is,' Nani said. 'She is leaving her parents' home and going to join a new family. Aunty and Uncle will be sad, too.'

'But, Nani, I thought that weddings were supposed to be happy.'

'Oh, but they are.' Nani smiled. 'I can still remember mine. Your Nana looked so handsome, I kept stealing peeks at him throughout the ceremony even though I wasn't supposed to.'

'Well,' said Jazeera after a pause. 'I hope that Salma Apa has a special day. I don't want her to be sad.'

'I hope so too,' said Nani.

As Jazeera stepped out of the car in front of the Civic Hall she noticed a buzz of excitement in the waiting crowd of relatives. Jazeera caught a few snatches of conversation.

'I think that she's coming . . .'

'Really, when . . .?'

'Do you think that she will?'

Jazeera thought that they were talking about the bride.

'Don't worry,' she said to the chatting adults. 'She's in the car behind us.'

A sleek car slid into the car park. Slowly the door opened and a gasp of amazement rippled through the assembled guests, even Jazeera held her breath. For it was not Salma Apa who stepped out of the car but Meena Praveena, the famous film actress.

'What is she doing here?' breathed Jazeera in wonder. Meena looked fabulous in a silken saree the colour of deep moonlight. Her loose hair hung in waves over her slim shoulders and the diamonds on her necklace and rings sparkled brilliantly as she waved to the crowd.

All heads turned towards the entrance of the car park. The bridal car arrived and everybody moved forwards to welcome Salma. Passing a smiling Meena, the bride was ushered inside the Civic Hall and the crowd outside settled down to wait for the arrival of the groom.

Jazeera looked across at the now silent group of people who were watching the film star with self-satisfied smiles on their faces. Jazeera inched over to them.

'Is Meena here for the wedding?' she asked, shyly.

'It looks like it.'

'I didn't know SHE was coming!'

'We didn't even know ourselves until this morning. Meena is a distant cousin of one of Kabir's aunts. She is over here to promote her new film *Diamond Thief*, so as there was a wedding in the family she was invited to come.'

'Wow!'

'Actually, we didn't think that she would really come, her schedule is pretty hectic.'

Jazeera danced back to Nani who was rocking baby Azra over her shoulder.

'It is Meena, Nani, it really is her.'

'Of course it is,' Nani said haughtily. 'I'd recognise her anywhere. Don't forget I've been in one of her films.'

Jazeera nudged her grandmother.

'Why don't you go up and introduce yourself to her?'

'What nonsense!' said Nani hastily, smoothing out invisible creases from Azra's frilly dress. 'What would Meena Praveena want to speak to an old woman like me for!'

But Jazeera could tell that secretly Nani would like to meet the star.

Dear Diary,

Salma Apa got married today. The wedding was fabulous. And you'll never guess what – Meena Praveena was there. She was so beautiful, much better than in her films. Meena even gave Salma Apa a present. It was a beautiful clock. Salma Apa was very surprised.

The best bit, though, was the photographs. When it was our turn to be photographed with the bride and groom, Salma Apa asked if Meena could be in the picture too. She stood next to Nani.

Nani wasn't going to say anything, so I told Meena that Nani had been in her last film as one of the extras in the crowd. That started them off! They talked about filming which made Nani's day. After the ceremony Meena had to leave to go and do a radio interview.

I am tired now, so many exciting things have happened today and it's very late. The wedding reception was brilliant. There were about 500 people and the hall had been decorated with huge red and white paper flowers. People threw streamers at each other until the dancefloor was a swirling mass of paper. Omar thought that was the best bit! He played in it for ages and kept getting trodden on by the dancers.

We had a disco and they had special flashing lights which made Kabir and Salma Apa's names come in a huge heart shape on the walls. I danced and danced until my feet hurt. Everybody liked my outfit, it was especially good when I twirled.

Salma looked so beautiful in her red saree. It was covered with millions of glittering sequins which sparkled in the lights when she and Kabir danced. The jewellery which Aunty Naseema brought from India looked good, especially the nose chain. It had ten tiny golden coins dangling from it, with 'S' and 'K' engraved in a love heart on each one. When I get married I would like to have a chain like that.

I'd better stop writing now. I was very worried that Salma Apa would be sad on her wedding day but because Meena Praveena came she was too excited to be sad. I was pleased that she had an extra special day.

The kettle sang shrilly to itself in the corner of the kitchen. Jazeera's mother sat calmly at the table feeding baby Azra while Jazeera and Omar squabbled over the last *paratha*.

There was a loud thud in the hallway. A minute later Jazeera's father appeared in the kitchen clutching a large bundle of letters. Smiling down at the children he sat at the table and began to sort through the mail.

'Oh look,' he said. 'The photos that I took at the wedding have arrived. That was quick!'

Everyone stopped whatever they were doing, except baby Azra, who continued to suck contentedly at her milk, and crowded around Jazeera's father. He ripped open the packet and took the shiny photographs out, one by one.

'Oh no, look at me in this one!'

'Mum, you've got your eyes closed here.'

'It's a pity that you chopped Kabir's head off this one, dear.'

'Hey, wow! Look at that!'

This last comment was directed at a photo of the family group standing around the bride and groom. Next to Salma and Nani stood the radiant figure of Meena Praveena. Everyone was smiling and looking very happy.

Dear Kurshid,

What a lovely time I have had. Weddings here are quite different from the ones in India. Even though it is summer, the whole wedding was indoors, in a community hall. It seemed strange not to be in the bride's home and not to have a procession.

And you'll never guess who I met! Meena Praveena, *she came to the wedding. Jazeera told her about us being in her film and I had such a nice chat to her. Meena told me to say 'hello' to you.*

Everybody was dressed very grandly in such beautiful sarees. Inside the hall it was like a little piece of India, even though the flowers were only paper. I was a bit chilly, though, and kept my cardigan on. I have to admit that I didn't care much for the music that everybody danced to afterwards, it was a bit loud! Salma told me that it was called Bhangra, *a mix of Punjabi and rock music!*

Do write and send me all your news.

Nani

Life became a whirlwind during the next few days as Aunty and Uncle prepared to fly back to India. Uncle needed to be back at his bangle shop and Aunty was rather anxious about the house being left unattended. Much to Jazeera's delight, it had been decided that Nani would stay on for five months for a holiday. Jazeera danced ecstatically around the kitchen when she heard the news and talked non-stop about the things that they could do together over the summer and the places they could visit.

Before all that there were letters to write and messages to be delivered to a myriad of old neighbours in India who were keen to hear news of the children and especially baby Azra. Most importantly, there were gifts to be bought.

Jazeera spent hours trawling the shops in the High Street, agonising over what to buy for her friend Ayisha. In the end she decided on a pair of fluffy purple slippers with satin bows and a book of school stories, as she knew that Ayisha liked reading.

As she stood in the queue at the bookshop Jazeera's face clouded over. Lines creased her face as she frowned.

'Nani,' she said quietly.

Soft eyes gazed enquiringly down at her under raised eyebrows.

'Nani, do you think that Anil would like a book?'

'Why, I'm sure he would,' Nani answered. 'He doesn't have any money for luxuries like books any more.'

'Look, there's one here called Amazing Facts about Your Body. If he wants to be a doctor, that would help him, wouldn't it?'

Nani tilted her head and chuckled.

'I'm sure he'd be delighted with that.'

Jazeera frowned as she counted the money in her purse. She had just enough money for the two books together, but nothing left over.

'It will mean that we can't go to Franco's for an ice cream, if I buy this now,' Jazeera said.

Nani looked at her steadily. 'I don't mind. We could go to the park instead.'

That decided it. Jazeera took the two books up to the counter and paid for them. Clutching her purchases, she turned to Nani. 'To the park it is, then!'

Nani's smile crinkled over her cheeks.

'You know, Jazeera, I think that this will probably be the first time that Anil has ever been given a book. He will be thrilled.'

1 August

Dear Kurshid,

Naseema and Salim will be returning with this letter. I have bought a radio for you. I hope that you can work out the instructions, they seem to be written in all languages even Chinese. Jazeera has bought a book for Anil, I hope that he likes it. How is he doing, does he get much time for his studies? You must encourage him all you can, he is such a clever boy.

Thank you for your letter, it was lovely to hear all your news. I'm glad to hear that you have found a reliable dhobi–wallah at last, here everybody does their own washing and ironing! Thank you for picking the mangoes from my garden. Can you make some nice mango pickle for me? You do make the best mango pickle that I have ever tasted.

Yesterday Jazeera and I went to visit her new school, it was very grand. There was a very wide wooden staircase in the hallway and the building was very old. The school was being used for a summer course but the kind lady in the office showed us around. They even have their own swimming pool. Jazeera was very taken by that. I think that she might enjoy going there if she passes the entrance exam.

I look forward to hearing your next letter.

Nani

4. Jazeera in Trouble

Dear Diary,
I hate Amy. She's such a goody-goody and she's always getting me into trouble. When I said that to Mummy she wanted to know what had happened on all the other times that Amy had got me into trouble. I couldn't think of anything right away, so Mummy said perhaps it wasn't true. Anyway, Mummy doesn't know everything. She even says that it was just as much my fault as Amy's, but I don't see how. The policeman has taken Amy home now, but I'm never going to speak to her again in my entire life.
It all happened when Nani and I went

into town. After we bought the presents we went to the park. On the way there we passed the library. I thought that she might like to see where the Urdu books were. While we were looking at them I felt a tap on my shoulder. It was Amy, she was in there with her mother. I told her that we were going to the park and she asked if she could come along too. Nani said that she would keep an eye on us both, so Amy's mum agreed. Amy likes to think that she is better than everyone else at doing things, so it was her fault really . . .

Jazeera and Amy led Nani out of the cool library building, over the crossing and into the park. Once inside the imposing gates, Amy called out, 'Bet you can't beat me to the pond.'

Before she had even finished the sentence she had set off with smooth, leggy strides in the direction of the murky water that served as a duck pond. Jazeera took off after her as soon

as she realised what was happening. She was at a disadvantage, though, having shorter legs and Amy won easily.

By the time Nani reached the pond the two girls were having a stone-throwing competition at the island in the centre of the pond.

'Bet you can't hit that old can over there,' Jazeera called.

Amy's stone sang through the air and landed with a twang on the discarded can. Immediately, she threw again and again, each time a perfect aim. Jazeera's shot went wide and plopped into the water missing the island altogether, never mind the can.

Having lost to Amy twice, Jazeera was determined to find something that she could win at. But Amy was agile and strong, everything that Jazeera suggested, Amy won easily.

Panting, and out of breath, the girls flopped down on the grass beside Nani's deckchair.

'You'll have to try harder, Jaz, if you want to beat me,' Amy grinned.

'I can beat you any day.'

'Not today, though.'

'I bet you, I can.'

Insects droned lazily around them and birds chirped in the branches of the tall elm trees overhead, but Jazeera was oblivious to the soothing sounds of summer.

'Anyway,' challenged Amy, 'I beat you in the end of term quiz.'

'Only by one, *and* you cheated.'

'I did not.'

'You did too. I saw you copying Moni.'

Jazeera felt heat rushing to her head. Amy got a bit big for her boots sometimes.

'I did not copy off Moni, I'm just better than you,' Amy countered.

'You are not, Amy. You can't play anything in music class except the tambourine!'

'Playing the piano isn't everything.'

'It's enough to get me into Highthorn, though.'

There, she had said it. She didn't want to go to Highthorn, and now she was using the school in an argument with her friend. One of the very friends she did not want to leave behind.

'Jazeera' Nani exclaimed, shooting a look of warning across to her furious granddaughter.

Jazeera felt flushed and angry. She didn't like being beaten by Amy, she didn't like Amy bragging about it and she didn't like being shown up in front of her Nani. She had to do something to show Amy once and for all. There had to be something that she could win at.

A gentle breeze stirred the leaves of the tall tree overhead and at once Jazeera knew what the bet would be.

'I bet I can climb higher up this tree than you can!' she challenged.

Before Nani could protest both girls were swinging their legs up and hooking them on to the lower branches. The tree was a sturdy one with plenty of leaves and it was often used for adventurous games by the local children. It grew high and tapered towards the top, so most of the playing was done on the lower branches. This dare, however, was to the top.

Jazeera and Amy scrambled frantically up and up, past the thick lower branches, over the stout middle branches and on towards the uppermost reaches of the tree. Neck and neck in the race, the two girls were so totally absorbed in winning the dare that they didn't notice the trunk getting slimmer and slimmer or the branches getting smaller and higher until Jazeera put her weight on to a branch which simply snapped beneath her. For a wild moment she lost her balance, her left leg kicked frantically trying to find a branch. The top of the tree swayed sickeningly under the girls' combined weight, like a pendulum.

Jazeera's scratched foot found a branch and, not daring to put her full weight on it, Jazeera froze to the tree. Beside her, Amy looked worried.

'I think we are equal on this one, Jaz, let's go down now.'

Jazeera nodded, her lips tightly pursed and screwed her eyes shut. Amy shuffled her weight and stretched gingerly backwards. Slowly, slowly she inched down until she was below Jazeera.

'Come on, Jaz, you can come down now.'

Hearing Amy call, Jazeera opened her eyes cautiously. She bent her head to see her friend but Amy was masked by a mass of silvery-green leaves. All Jazeera saw was the great rushing distance to the ground. A tiny figure below waved and shouted frantically but no sound came to Jazeera's ears. The yellowing summer grass of the park swam mistily before her eyes as Jazeera's head spun, dizzily. In terror she clung even tighter to the bowing trunk beside her and her fingernails dug ever deeper into the tree's soft bark.

Jazeera was afraid. Afraid to stay where she was on the delicate branches. Afraid to move in case another branch snapped under her weight and sent her hurtling to the bottom. Afraid even to open her eyes in case the ground engulfed her. All she could do was stay frozen to the spot. Her arms ached with holding on so tightly, her breath came in painful rasps.

Because her eyes were so tightly

closed, Jazeera didn't see the tiny white-robed figure hurry across the park to the gates. She didn't see the figure fumble in the telephone booth, or come scurrying anxiously back to the foot of the tree. It wasn't until the wail of a siren pierced the air that Jazeera realised someone was coming to rescue her.

By the time the gleaming red fire-engine had parked beneath the tree and the heavy-coated fire-fighters were expertly extending their ladder, quite a crowd had gathered around the bottom.

A fire-fighter scaled the ladder and reached out to touch Jazeera's shoulder. Jazeera opened her eyes and tears of relief sprang into them as she saw the friendly face.

'Come along now, easy does it,' the fire-fighter coaxed.

Jazeera released fear-cramped fingers from the tree trunk. A surge of sickness attacked her stomach as she hung, momentarily suspended in the air between the tree and the ladder. Then she was safe. The fire-fighter's strong arms supported her and she was carried to the ground.

The instant her feet touched the ground the blue dizziness left her and Jazeera trembled violently with relief. Nani and Amy pounced on her and hugged her, glad that she was safe.

It was a policeman who broke up the crowd, thanked the fire-crew and offered Nani and the girls a lift home. There, around the kitchen table, Jazeera and Amy had to repeat their stories to the group of assembled adults.

'Jazeera, how could you?' her mother said sternly. 'Look at all the trouble you have caused.'

Jazeera stared glumly at the table. After having such a terrible experience, here she was being told off.

'Well,' said her father glaring at her with wide eyes. 'Don't you have something to say?'

A hard lump formed at the back of Jazeera's throat, her face felt hot and prickly with sweat. Her lips trembled. Why should she apologise? Why should she!

Jazeera looked at the expectant faces around her.

'It wasn't my fault,' she blurted. 'It was Amy, she started it all.'

Jazeera's finger flew out accusingly at her bewildered friend.

'Why don't you make *her* say sorry?'

Jazeera jumped up and ran out of the kitchen, threw herself down on her bed and cried until she fell into an exhausted sleep.

19 August

Dear Kurshid,

Thank you for your letter, I am so glad that you liked the radio. It is a good job that Anil was there to help you to set it up. I told you that he was clever.

What excitement there has been here, I can't tell you! I had such a fright. Jazeera and a friend had a silly bet and climbed a tall tree. Jazeera went and got herself stuck at the top! I had to call the fire brigade and you wouldn't believe how difficult it is to make a telephone call. There was no man in the box to help me. I didn't know what to do. The instructions for calling the emergency services were written on the wall but somebody had scribbled on them so I couldn't read it. It was very lucky that a young lady came by and helped me. It's actually quite easy when you know how.

Can you imagine how worried I was?

I thought that Jazeera might let go and fall, crashing to the ground at any minute. Fortunately the fire brigade came quickly. They put a ladder up to the tree and brought my naughty granddaughter down safely.

Jazeera has been in a state of shock and, of course, everybody has told her off so she has been very upset. I think that she and I should have a little chat and soon!

Yours

Nani

Yawning, Jazeera pushed the shopping trolley slowly down the regimented aisles of the supermarket. Nani dawdled behind, gazing at the neat shelves crammed with enticing tins and packets. It amazed her that there were so many different tins of peas! What was the difference, which one should she buy? Back in India everything was bought fresh from the bazaar, it was so much easier.

Jazeera was silent as she manoeuvred the shiny trolley between the other shoppers and on towards the bread counter. She was still smarting from the thorough telling-off she had received from her parents. They had been furious about the tree incident and had stood over Jazeera while she wrote a grudging letter of apology to the fire brigade and the policeman for all the trouble she had caused. That had hurt, especially as it was all Amy's fault.

What hurt more was the fact that all day Nani had been strangely silent on the subject. Jazeera expected her grandmother to say something, but no, she had simply suggested that the two of them should go and fetch the groceries. Jazeera wanted Nani to say something so that she could protest her innocence, but Nani just got on with the business of shopping and Jazeera was left to her own thoughts.

And these thoughts were none too pleasant. Jazeera still felt flushed and angry whenever she thought about being told off, but now and again memories popped, unbidden, into her mind. Memories of exactly who had been taunting who, in the park. Who it was that had suggested the climb in the first place.

'It was Amy's fault,' she thought bitterly, trying to convince herself that it was. 'She thinks that she's so clever.'

'Jazeera, which of these tins is the best?'

Nani looked puzzled, holding out two brands of beans.

Jazeera sighed.

'I don't think either is better, they're just different makes.'

'But surely,' said Nani frowning, 'this one is better because it is bigger.'

'Not really, Nani. The smaller one is cheaper.'

'And look!' said Nani, extracting a third tin. 'This one has a special offer. Which one should we choose?'

'Oh, I don't know,' snapped Jazeera,

hating to be bothered by these petty problems when she had much bigger ones revolving in her mind. 'It doesn't matter which one. They are all pretty much the same, inside.'

Nani put all three tins of beans down carefully in the trolley, much to Jazeera's surprise.

'Now don't you think they're just like you and your friends,' Nani suggested, a hint of a smile playing in her eyes.

'Nani! We're nothing like tins of beans!'

'No, of course not. But, like the tins, you are all a bit different on the outside, but really the same on the inside.'

'Nani, it was Amy who . . .' Jazeera began desperately.

With a swift swish of her saree, Nani turned and marched purposefully down another aisle, her eyes scanning the shelves for the next item on her list. Jazeera was left to trail uncomfortably behind. As much as she hated it, Jazeera realised that Nani was right. Slowly she

approached the bent figure rummaging for the ripest onions on the rack.

'It wasn't really right of me to be jealous of Amy's running and things, was it?'

Nani continued with her foraging and Jazeera sensed that there was more to it than that. She looked down contritely.

'I guess I shouldn't have shown off about Highthorn, either,' she added quietly.

Nani straightened up and smiled.

'I'm glad that you can see that now,' she said, tossing a bag of onions into the trolley. 'You know as well as I do that Amy was wrong to taunt you, but that doesn't excuse your behaviour.'

Jazeera stared solidly at the tiled floor, her vision wobbling as tears floated into her eyes. Nani put her arm around her, comfortingly.

'We are each special in our own way, you know. Just because you are gifted at piano playing doesn't make you a better person than any of your friends. You have a right to be proud of your talent, but you must not become big-headed. We are all special in the sight of God. Remember that, Jazeera.'

Jazeera nodded.

'Come,' said Nani. 'We have more things to buy.'

Dear Diary,

I went round to Amy's today. At first I wasn't sure that she was going to speak to me but her mother let me in so she had to. It was really, really hard but I thought about what Nani had said to me and I said sorry to Amy. She was cool about it and said that she was sorry too. Apparently her parents had given her grief over it all too. At least now we're friends again. Amy said that Nani had been very calm and sensible and it was all down to her that I got rescued at all. She suggested that we get Nani a present or something to say thank you. It was then that I had my BIG IDEA. I don't know yet if it will work and I will need a lot of help but Amy likes it, so I'm going to give it a try.

By the way, I got a letter from Anil today. His writing is much neater than mine. He wanted to say how much he appreciated the book. He is keeping it in a place of honour beside the family shrine, which I think is a bit much since it's not a holy book or anything. Still, at least he liked it.

Amy, Moni and I are going swimming tomorrow. Maybe we'll take Nani, she hasn't seen our leisure centre yet. Omar wants to come but I said no because he's too much of a baby and he can't swim without armbands on. I'm glad that Amy and I are friends again.

5. Going . . . Going . . . Gone

18 September

Dear Kurshid,

The summer seems to have flown by. It seems like only yesterday that I arrived, and now here it is, September already and the children are back at school.

I am lonely without Jazeera. She has been my constant companion, taking me to the seaside, walking and exploring the streets and lanes nearby. The sun here is so soft and refreshing that I feel ten years younger. Now the leaves on the trees are turning all shades of orange and gold and the evenings are getting chillier. There is such a big difference between the seasons in this country.

I have just received your letter. How exciting that your son–in–law is building a house next to yours. You will be lucky to have your grandchildren so close to you all the time. I am pleased that little Anil is able to earn some money by helping the bricklayers. It is such a shame that he cannot be at school.

I'd better close now, the children will be home from school and I do love to hear about their day.

Yours,

Nani

Jazeera and Omar tumbled excitedly into the kitchen ahead of their mother, both talking at once, and flung their school bags on the nearest chair. Nani, with a sleeping Azra cradled in her arms, put her finger to her lips to shush the noise.

Ignoring her, both Jazeera and Omar darted to the fridge and grabbed for the milk at the same time. Being taller than her brother, Jazeera was able to elbow him out of the way.

'Aw . . . Mum,' Omar wailed. 'Just because she's older, why does she have to get the drinks first. She'll take it all.'

'Stop it, children,' interrupted their mother wearily, leaning across and taking the carton from their squabbling hands. 'You can both have some.' She poured out equal amounts into two tall glasses.

Baby Azra squirmed on Nani's lap and opened her deep brown eyes. Her tiny forehead creased into a frown.

'Atishoo!' She spluttered through her gummy mouth, eyes wide with startled surprise.

'Oh no,' sighed her mother, picking the baby up. 'I hope that you're not getting a cold.'

'Sit down,' said Nani. 'Let me make you a cup of tea.'

As the old lady shuffled to the kettle she felt her nose tickle and before she knew it, 'Atishoo!' a sneeze popped out, then another and another. Jazeera handed her a box of tissues.

'It looks as though you've caught one too, Nani.'

'I don't know, I've never had one before,' Nani sniffed.

Nani made the tea, then took her cup and went to sit down beside Jazeera.

'Now then, Zeeraji, tell me what you've been doing at school, today. How did your music lesson go?'

'Oh fine.' Jazeera shrugged.

'But guess what, Nani!' Jazeera continued, her eyes bright with excitement. 'We're going to have a charity fair this term. There's going to be a competition to see which class can raise the most money. We spent ages discussing it today.'

'That sounds interesting,' said Nani. 'Who are you going to give the money to?'

'We can't decide. Mr Foster said that we should concentrate on raising money first and think about who to give it to, later.'

'Quite right!'

'Omar told me that the infants are going to have a jumble sale, well, I suppose the mums will be doing most of it. And Class 4 are going to cook something that they can sell. We couldn't decide what to do, but it has to be something extra special.

'Brent Cooper suggested that people could pay a pound to throw rotten tomatoes at Mr Foster, but Mr Foster wasn't too keen on that idea. Then Mr Foster said that perhaps we should do something really challenging, like a sponsored silence, but we all said, "no way," to that!'

'So what are you going to do?' Nani asked, interested.

'Well, in the end it was Moni's idea. She and Amy were swapping comics and she said that we could all bring in our old books and comics and sell them off.'

'Oh, a book stall.'

'No, Nani, better than that. Mr Foster said that if we collected enough books perhaps we could have an auction. That way we can make sure that we sell everything and we can each take it in turns to be the auctioneer.'

Nani sneezed, then smiled.

'That sounds like a good idea.'

'It's brilliant, Nani. I'm off to see which of my books I can give. Then maybe we can ask the other people in the building. The more we get the better.'

Jazeera skipped happily off to the bookshelf in her bedroom while Nani plucked another tissue from the box and gave her nose a vigorous blow.

Later that evening Jazeera and Nani climbed up and down the stairs, knocking on all the neighbours' doors. Everybody was very helpful and pleased to hear about the auction.

'It's so good to see the youngsters

doing something positive with their time,' said the lady from the basement flat as she parted with an armful of paperback romances. Jazeera and Nani put them all carefully into two plastic bags and climbed up to the next flat.

Nani thought that it was the weight of the bags of books that made her arms and back ache. As more and more books were added to the collection, Nani found it harder and harder to climb the stairs. Her head was starting to spin and, to make matters worse, some of the books were dusty which made her sneeze even more. By the time they reached Flat 5, she was exhausted.

'Last one,' whispered Jazeera as she pressed the buzzer. 'We might not get anything here. Mr Holden is a grumpy old man. He has never liked us since the time Omar left the taps on in the bathroom and his flat got flooded.

A soft shuffle was heard, and a fierce-looking, white-haired man poked his head around the door.

'Hello,' said Jazeera, politely.

Mr Holden ignored her and looked at the stooping figure of Nani. His expression softened.

'Can I help you?' he asked.

'We're collecting books for a charity auction,' explained Jazeera. But the old man paid no attention to her, whatsoever. He looked down at their bulging carrier bags.

''Ere, you're not selling anything, are

you, 'coz I don't want any.' Nani smiled, gathering her breath.

'No,' she sniffed, 'we're collecting. Collecting books for charity.'

'Oh!' Mr Holden said, obviously relieved. 'Why didn't you say so, come on in then.'

'But I . . .' protested Jazeera.

Mr Holden took Nani's arm and led her to an upright chair in his hallway.

'There you are. You sit right there. You look exhausted.'

Nani was quite glad of a chance to sit down.

'Now then, what's this you're collecting?' The old man smiled at Nani. So Nani explained everything while Jazeera stood fuming beside her. Mr Holden nodded, then disappeared into one of the rooms. He returned a moment later with a leather-backed book that looked very old.

'It was my wife's,' he said. 'She read a lot, but I got rid of most of them years ago when I moved here.' He pressed the book into Nani's hands.

'Oh but we can't take this if it's of sentimental value to you,' Nani exclaimed.

'Nonsense, she would be delighted that it's going to a good cause.' He flashed a smile at Nani. 'Anyway, you remind me of her. Are you living here, now?' he asked.

'Just staying for a holiday,' Nani replied.

Jazeera tugged at her Nani's saree.

'Well, you must allow me to take you to our community day centre, sometime.'

'Thank you,' said Nani, struggling to get to her feet. Mr Holden leapt forward and took her elbow, escorting her to the door.

'I'll call for you one day in the week,' he smiled before closing the door on them.

'Nani!' Jazeera exploded. 'He fancies you!'

'Don't be silly, Jazeera,' Nani said, pushing a strand of hair absently out of her eyes. She really did feel extraordinarily tired. 'He's just a pleasant old man.'

'Humpf,' muttered Jazeera. 'He wasn't very generous, though. One measly book, and it's dead boring too. Nobody's going to want to buy that.' Jazeera shoved the book into the carrier bag along with all the others and followed Nani up the stairs and back home.

Dear Diary,

I am very worried about Nani. She has been ill for over a week now. Aunty Rehanna is coming round tonight with some homeopathic medicine. Maybe that'll work.

We have collected loads of books now. They are all in a big pile in the corner of the classroom. Mr Foster says that next week we will divide them into 'lots', so that six magazines or four paperbacks will make a 'lot' and they will be sold together. We will each have five 'lots' to sell and Brent Cooper brought in a little hammer so we have all been practising at being auctioneers.

In art class we have been making a banner saying BOOK AUCTION in old-fashioned letters. The fair is next week and we are sure that the auction will make more money than any other class. Moni says that she will open all her bids at five pounds, that way she will make lots of money as the prices go up. I think she is crazy, nobody will pay that much for a bunch of old comics.

I do hope that Nani is better in time for the fair. At least Nani being in bed has given me lots of time to get everything ready, mind you, I've had to rely on Uncle and Daddy a lot because my entrance exam is coming up soon and I have to do a lot of piano practice after school.

Jazeera and Nani pushed their way into the brightly lit school hall already pulsing with throngs of excited people. A hubbub of confusion reigned as a horde of experienced old ladies elbowed their way to the front of the jumble-sale tables. Above their bobbing heads Jazeera could make out her mother and Salma Apa among the team of parent helpers frantically serving the onslaught of bargain hunters.

To the left, Class 4's food stall sent delicious aromas wafting across the crowded hall, but most of the tastiest food had already been bought. Jazeera

81

and Nani had come late because Nani was still weak from her bout of flu and Jazeera had wanted her to be there in the afternoon for the auction.

Jazeera led Nani around the stalls. They guessed how many Smarties there were in a jar, they stuck a pin in a treasure map and they bought stacks of raffle tickets. Eventually they found themselves by the stage where an interested crowd was studying the books laid out in lot order ready for the auction. One man in a grey raincoat seemed particularly interested and studied every title carefully.

Jazeera felt a tingle of excitement rustle up and down her spine when at two o'clock Mr Foster announced that the book auction would begin. He kicked off with lot 1, an assorted collection of travel books which sold quite quickly to a well-dressed woman at the front with horn-rimmed spectacles.

Soon the attention of the crowd drifted from the now devastated jumble-sale tables to the stage. As each child from Jazeera's class stood up to the microphone to sell their lots, the crowd increased. More and more people began to join in the bidding and Jazeera was surprised at how well the books sold. A group of top infants bid against each other for the bundles of comics for 50p and some of the mothers bought the romantic novels for two pounds but strangely enough it was the lady in the smart suit who bought the most.

When it was Jazeera's turn, she stepped up on to the stage close to the microphone and picked up the little hammer.

'Ladies and gentleman,' she began in a loud, clear voice.

'Here we have lot 35, a superb collection of crime stories.'

Mr Foster held the bundle of books aloft so that the crowd could see.

'If we have any budding detectives out there shall we start the bidding at say, one pound . . .'

Jazeera sold the crime novels eventually to Kabir for £3.35 so she was very pleased. Swiftly she dealt with lots 36, 37 and 38. Then came her last lot, lot 39.

Lot 39 was a single book. The one that Mr Holden had given to Jazeera, well, given to Nani actually. Mr Foster had decided to put it on its own because there wasn't anything else quite like it.

Jazeera waited for the crowd to quieten before she announced lot 39.

'Now, ladies and gentlemen, take a good look at lot 39. This is a handsome volume of *Shuttlethwait's Anthology*'. She stumbled slightly over the long, unfamiliar words. Jazeera didn't think that it looked handsome at all, she thought that it looked boring, but Mr Foster had told her what to say.

'How shall we begin the bidding? Do I have an opening offer?'

'One pound,' came the smart-suited lady, quickly.

Nani smiled. She thought that the posh lady had bought too much already and as she hadn't bought anything herself, she added: 'Two pounds.'

'Three pounds,' came back the lady rather swiftly.

'Five pounds,' came a voice from the back of the room.

Jazeera was amazed. None of the other lots had sold for five pounds, even the one that had seven encyclopaedias in.

'Going for five pounds to . . .' Jazeera began raising the hammer.

'Ten pounds,' said the smart-suited lady, rapidly.

'Fifteen,' said the voice.

Jazeera was so surprised that she almost forgot to see who was bidding from the back of the room. It was the little gentleman in the grey coat. Before she had recovered from her shock the lady took off her horn-rimmed glasses and with a flourish, called 'One hundred pounds.'

A gasp of amazement rippled audibly through the assembled crowd and Jazeera nearly dropped her hammer. She couldn't have heard correctly.

'What?' she croaked.

'Two hundred pounds,' called the man from the back, calmly.

'Three hundred.'

As news spread throughout the school, of the high bidding going on at the auction, more and more people flocked into the hall to see what would happen.

'Eight hundred pounds,' cried the lady, now frowning at the volume held high in Mr Foster's hand.

'ONE THOUSAND POUNDS,'

thundered the grey-coated man from the back.

A thick silence settled on the crowd in the hall as the words echoed in everyone's ears. Even the smart-suited lady was quiet. Visibly deflated, she shook her head.

'A . . . a thousand pounds,' stammered Jazeera, too stunned to say anything else. Out of the corner of her eye she saw Nani waving her arm up and down. Oh yes! Jazeera rapped the hammer, sharply on the desk.

'Sold to the man in the grey coat for one thousand pounds.'

The tension was broken and the applause hit the roof. Mr Foster reached forwards to help Jazeera down from the stage.

'Well done,' he beamed.

Just then the little man appeared at the front waving a cheque. He picked up the book that he had just bought and stroked it lovingly.

'It's a first edition, you know,' he said.

'Very valuable. She was going to sell it abroad.' The man nodded in the direction of the suited lady. 'But I want it for my collection.' The man smiled at Jazeera. 'I'll look after it, don't you worry.'

'Well, Jazeera,' smiled Mr Foster. 'We've certainly won the competition for collecting the most money after that!'

Brent Cooper took his place on the stage and announced lot 40. 'Would anybody like to start the bidding at a hundred pounds for this neat collection of *Good Housekeeping* magazines . . .'

Everybody laughed.

6. Winter Wonderland

31 October

Dear Kurshid,

You'll never guess how much money Jazeera's class managed to raise at their charity fair. It was over 10,000 rupees! Can you imagine it. It must be more than you and I have raised in our entire lives! Mind you, most of it came from the sale of one book. It was a valuable first edition given by a gentleman who lives in a flat below us.

When they realised how much money had been raised Jazeera and her teacher went round to Mr Holden's flat and offered to give him half the money back. He probably never realised how much it was worth. But he very kindly let them keep it all. He said that he didn't need it. Now that he was old he would like the money to go towards helping someone else. How many people do you know who would do that?

The weather is miserable and windy now. I am feeling much better after my flu but I still get very tired. The constant chill gets me down. I suppose that I am imagining things because I am an old lady, but everybody is behaving very strangely. When I come into a room they all stop talking and there is an uncomfortable silence. Then they start to talk about something else. They think that I haven't noticed, just because I don't say anything, but I wasn't born yesterday.

Yours

Nani

Dear Diary,

Everything is going according to plan . . .

'Have you got them yet?' Jazeera asked urgently.

'Yes, yes,' said her father. 'Don't worry.'

'But what about . . .'

Nani opened the kitchen door.

'I haven't interrupted anything, have I?' she asked curiously.

'No, not at all,' said Jazeera's father, standing up. 'Why don't you two go off to the town centre, see the shops. They're all decked out for Christmas now.'

'That would be nice,' said Jazeera. 'You never know what you might be able to find.'

'What do you mean, Daddy?'

'Didn't you know, it's Nani's birthday soon.'

Jazeera stared at him, her mouth wide open with annoyed surprise.

'Nonsense,' flustered Nani. 'I don't want Jazeera to spend her money on me. I'm just an old lady.'

'Well, I'd better be going,' Jazeera's father laughed. Luckily he left before he saw Jazeera's face.

Outside, tiny slivers of snow drifted lazily down from dark clouds, they settled on hats, scarves and the backs of coats, glistening momentarily before vanishing into a mass of dampness. The air was scissor sharp with cold and billowing with the cloudy breath of hundreds of busy shoppers.

Even though it was still early, the light was fading and the shoppers pulled their coats around themselves in an attempt to keep warm as they hurried from one welcoming doorway to the next.

Jazeera and Nani stood in front of a brightly lit window staring in awe at the magical scene spread before them.

'I've never seen anything like it before,' breathed Nani, as her eyes followed the steady rocking movements of a purple fairy on a trapeze. Below the

fairy there was a mountain of toys surrounded by fake snow which glistened brightly under the strong lights.

'Come on,' said Jazeera, tugging at Nani's coat with her gloved hand. 'Look at this one.'

Behind the next window was a yet more splendid scene with a plump red-coated figure in the act of tumbling down a tall chimney while his upturned sack spilled presents over the shining red roof.

Totally absorbed in the unfolding scenes before them, Jazeera and Nani forgot about their frozen toes and numb noses as they wandered slowly around the store windows. Some windows had boring things like plates and glasses tied with glossy red bows, but most had some sort of entrancing moving figure. Jazeera's favourite was the flying reindeer against a background of spinning stars. She had been learning a song about a reindeer at school.

They made their way back to the entrance again. By this time a group of carol singers had gathered in front of the doorway. Well muffled up against the wintery onslaught from above, they stood beneath the massive Christmas tree and poured out jaunty music in great steaming breaths.

The snowflakes drizzled faster and faster. All the shoppers entering the store were now sprinkled with a fine white layer of snow, like sugar-coated cakes. Shaking the soggy snow from the folds of their umbrellas Jazeera and Nani walked up to the inviting glow of the entrance.

Inside the store a blanket of sweet-smelling warmth wrapped itself around them. Tall Christmas trees laden with golden tinsel and dripping with baubles stood above every counter like a colourful army of giants. Everywhere was sparkling with glitter and magic. Nani stopped and sniffed at the perfume counters. A glamorous lady gave Nani a spray with an expensive perfume and Nani insisted on smelling her wrist every five minutes after that.

'Would you like to meet Father Christmas, Nani?' giggled Jazeera.

'Well I never!' said Nani. But all the same she went up and shook the jolly figure by the hand and accepted a balloon with the store's name on from his assistant. Jazeera was very pleased with the balloon.

'I can put that to good use,' she muttered.

Nani's head was spinning with bewilderment at the heat, lights, noise and sparkle as they stepped into the bustling Cosmetic department.

'Just a minute, Nani,' said Jazeera mysteriously. 'Can you wait here for me? I won't be long.'

Jazeera left Nani looking at a rainbow of lipsticks while she darted furtively around a corner. By the time she returned, Nani had selected two bright-red lipsticks for Aunty and Mrs Khan,

along with matching nail polish.

On their way out Nani had another squirt of the perfume on her other wrist this time.

'What did you buy, *beyti*?' Nani asked.

'Nothing much,' said Jazeera, carefully holding a small bag behind her back. Nani didn't ask any more questions, she guessed what her little granddaughter was up to. Or at least she thought she did.

The next morning when Jazeera awoke she felt a strange tingle of excitement creep along her spine. She couldn't understand why. It was cold in the bedroom despite the central heating and the air seemed to be fresher, more invigorating than usual.

Jazeera got up and looked out of the window. What a sight met her eyes! The world had turned white overnight. It was like waking up in wonderland. Her normally dreary view of rooftops and telephone wires was totally transformed.

Nani sat up in bed sleepily. She rubbed her eyes then stared in wonder.

'The world has put new clothes on,' she gasped. 'It all looks so different.'

It did indeed. It looked pure and fresh. But more importantly it looked inviting. Jazeera just *had* to go out and play in it.

She dressed with lightning speed and wolfed down her breakfast. Omar had woken and demanded to go out too.

'Don't be too long, Jazeera,' called her mother. 'Remember, you are going for your piano lesson this morning.'

Finally, Nani was ready, wrapped up in her borrowed black overcoat and scarf. The three of them set off into wonderland.

Stepping outside, the first thing that Nani noticed was the icy air which rushed into her lungs catching her by surprise and almost making her choke. She had never breathed such coldness before. The second thing was that snow was unstable, it cracked and shifted underneath her feet. Nani found that she had to grip Jazeera's shoulders at first to balance herself but soon she got the hang of it.

Omar raced ahead while Jazeera helped Nani to the small back garden which they shared with the other residents. Actually it was quite hard to walk through the drifts of deep, fluffy snow that were piled against the sides of the building and once they were in the garden, it was impossible to tell where the path was. The whole garden was blanketed with smooth, white snow, peppered with deep footprints where Omar had dashed in an excited frenzy.

'Let's build a snowman, Jaz,' he cried, rushing off once more.

'How?' said Jazeera, her eyes shining with excitement.

But it didn't matter. The three of them gathered handfuls of pure white snow and patted them together to make a little mound which grew bigger and bigger very slowly.

Flushed and excited, Nani's gloved hand was patting a respectable handful on to the heap when footsteps were heard creaking through the snow. Jazeera and Omar in the far side of the garden stood up. Looking up, Nani saw Salma Apa and Kabir, dressed in wellingtons and heavy winter jackets.

'Hello,' Salma Apa called cheerfully.

Omar rushed forward at lightning speed and patted more snow on to the mound.

'We're making a snowman and it's going to be the biggest snowman in the world,' he announced.

'Well, I'm afraid that you're going to

have to work a bit harder than that!' said Kabir, squatting down and gesturing towards the pile of snow. 'Now, if you want to make a really big snowman, the best thing to do is this.'

He bent forwards and scooped some snow into his hand. Then with the other hand he patted it into a ball. Picking up some more snow, he patted that on to the ball, too. In no time at all the ball was really quite big.

'All you have to do is put it on to the ground and roll it.'

Pushing it gently along, Kabir demonstrated how easily the ball picked up the snow, leaving behind frosted blades of deep green grass. Omar soon got the hang of the technique and began rolling giant snowballs all over the garden. When they were the right size Salma and Kabir lifted them on to the mound, then Nani and Jazeera patted extra snow into the spaces to make the snowman's body.

'I never thought that snow could be so

much fun,' panted Nani, patting bits of now-gritty snow into place.

'Ah,' said Salma Apa. 'But if we had it all the time, like the Eskimos, we wouldn't think that it was so great.'

Nani shivered as she gazed up at the tree-frosted skyline. 'It looks pretty in the sunshine, doesn't it? So delicate and so light, yet deep down it is hard, tough as nails, a deceptive playfellow.'

'It's certainly cold,' agreed Kabir. 'Plenty of people dread this weather. And you'd best be careful, Nani, you won't be used to it.'

Nani nodded. Already icy crystals were seeping through her gloves and making her fingers itch. The snowman was almost finished. Most of the snow on the small lawn had been used up. Omar found some stones, which were pressed into a broad grin on the wobbly head, and Jazeera stuck on a couple of fir cones for eyes.

'I think that it's time to go in now,' called Salma Apa. So, leaving their new creation to stand sentinel and bareheaded under the pale winter sun, the family left the wreckage of the garden behind. As they stamped the snow from their boots they could smell the spicy warmth of their dinner.

'Perhaps it will snow some more,' suggested Omar. 'Then we could build another snowman.'

Nani looked at him kindly.

'You could,' she said. 'But you would have to get somebody else to help you. One snowman in a lifetime is quite enough for this old Nani.'

7. *Time to Go*

'Settle down, class,' shouted Mr Foster.
'I can't even hear myself think.'

The class quietened at once.

'Now then, as you all know, as a result
of Jazeera's incredible sale at the book
auction we have raised a grand total of
one thousand and seventy four pounds.

'Yeah! Yippee!'

The class broke out into a chorus
of shrieks, yells and general desk-
thumping. Mr Foster let it continue for a
moment before putting up his hand for
quiet.

'Well done, everybody. It was a
splendid effort all round. And later
today the head will present you with the

charity fair shield. We will be able to display it on the wall above the book corner for the rest of the year. I think that it's going to be a long time before any class beats that total.'

The whole class shuffled in their seats, excitedly.

'The next question,' Mr Foster continued, 'is what to do with the money. Before we can accept the shield we have to decide who will benefit from our efforts. Any ideas, anyone?'

Everyone frowned and thought hard.

'What about giving it to the blind, sir?'

'Good idea,' said Mr Foster. 'But I happen to know that the Infants will be donating their proceeds to that charity. Perhaps we shouldn't all give to the same place.'

'What about that home for the mentally handicapped?' Brent Cooper suggested.

'Sir, we gave to them last year,' Moni chipped in. 'Can't we think of something else? Something more unusual?'

'Yes,' everyone agreed.

'I was thinking,' said Mr Foster perching on the edge of his desk, 'as we raised our money through selling books, perhaps it would be nice to support some sort of educational charity.'

The class sat blankly. It was a reasonable enough suggestion but they couldn't think of anything.

'Come on,' said Mr Foster desperately, 'we have to think of something.'

A thought popped into Jazeera's head. She dismissed it but it wouldn't go away. So she thought about it some more then she decided to tell everyone her idea.

'Sir,' she said putting up her hand. 'I know of a boy in India. He's very clever but his father was killed in a storm last year and his school got washed away. He wants to be a doctor but now he can't afford to go to school. He has to work doing odd jobs in people's houses. Couldn't we help someone like him?'

Mr Foster's eyes lit up.

'Do you know,' he said, 'I have heard of schemes where you can sponsor a child in a developing country through their education.'

He looked up at the ceiling and did a few calculations in his head.

'I think that we would have just enough money to do that for this boy and have enough money left over to buy him some text books. What do you say, class?'

They all nodded in agreement.

'What's his name?'

'What does he look like?'

'Where does he live?'

A flood of questions poured out and Jazeera had to stand up at the front and tell them all everything that Nani had told her about Anil.

'Good,' said Mr Foster finally. 'If your grandmother can take some photographs of Anil when she returns to India and get some family details, we can put up a display on the wall.'

Jazeera skipped out of school that day into the sharp December air and thought about how pleased Nani would be to hear the news. But Nani would have to wait. Jazeera was going to be late home today, she had some errands to do. Jazeera saw her mother standing by the gates holding Omar's hand. Together they turned and walked towards the brilliantly lit shops.

4 December

Dear Kurshid,
Jazeera sat her entrance exam for the music school yesterday. She was very nervous, I could tell, but it doesn't seem to have affected her playing because the principal telephoned Mrs Levin, the headmistress at Jazeera's school, this afternoon. They will be offering Jazeera a scholarship place for next year.

We are all delighted with the news, of course, but when I suggested to Mohammed that we should throw a party to celebrate, he was strangely reluctant. He said that they were too busy! What kind of father is 'too busy' to congratulate his own daughter properly. I was very angry with him and I haven't spoken to him all day.

Actually no one is speaking to me much. The whole family seems to be preoccupied. It's as though they are trying to avoid me. I have been here for five months now and I think that maybe I have outstayed my welcome. Perhaps, in a way, it's a good thing that I am coming home next week.

I have missed our little chats on your verandah but I will see you again very soon.

Yours

Nani

Nani sat sleepily in front of the fire, half watching an old Meena Praveena film. She had seen it before but she thought that she had better stay out of everyone's way. They were all busy again today. The old lady felt uncomfortable and in the way.

Jazeera's mother bustled in.

'I met the postman downstairs, here's a letter for you.' She handed Nani a white envelope bearing three familiar Indian stamps. It was a birthday card from Nani's friend Mrs Khan.

'How nice of her to have remembered,' hinted Nani. But Jazeera's mother pretended not to hear. She hurried off into the kitchen to make the lunch.

Nani decided to be daring. She put the card up on the mantelpiece, right next to the photograph of Meena Praveena at the wedding. Nobody paid the slightest bit of attention to it.

'Come and sit over here, Zeeraji,' Nani called as Jazeera emerged from the kitchen.

Jazeera turned distractedly. 'Sorry, Nani, I'm a bit busy at the moment.' She vanished quickly into the bathroom.

'Oh,' Nani said to the empty room.

Dejectedly Nani got up and wandered into the bedroom that she was sharing with Jazeera. She might as well start her packing, there was nothing else to do. While gathering her things, Nani noticed that the black and white photograph of Jazeera's Nana was missing. She had taken it out of its frame to put the wedding photograph in.

'That was a mistake,' Nani thought crossly as she rummaged desperately in all the drawers. She was beginning to think that it was a mistake to have come here at all.

The pale winter sun finally admitted defeat and sank dejectedly behind a curtain of thick black clouds. Nani closed her suitcase and, looking out of the window, she saw two huge drops of rain splash, and then slowly slide down the pane. For a while she watched the steady descent of the rain as it disappeared silently on to the inky black ground below.

'Nani,' called cheery voices.

It was Salma and Kabir. They stood in the doorway, a fine layer of moisture clinging to their coats and hair.

'Come on, Nani,' said Kabir. 'We've come to take you out for a drive.'

'At this time of night,' protested Nani.

'Yes, come on,' said Salma

encouragingly. 'We're going to take you to see some friends.'

'Well, this is a nice surprise,' Nani said loudly, hoping that some of the family could hear. 'Is anyone else coming?'

Jazeera shook her head. 'Not tonight, Nani, we're busy.'

Nani got ready in silence.

'Bye, everyone,' called Salma and Kabir. 'See you later.'

'Bye, Nani,' Jazeera's mother called.

This time Nani pretended not to have heard.

Nani was unusually quiet as the car glided past streets of silent, grey houses shrouded in a cloak of steel-grey rain. She shivered in the gloom of the car and pulled her coat closer around her shoulders.

Outside, the winter rain fell faster and faster. Nani paid no attention to where they were driving. Soon she would be back in India where at least it would be warm. At first the winter weather had been new and exciting, now it seemed to sap her energy with its all-consuming cold and Nani could almost feel herself shrinking inside her body.

Kabir stopped the car and Nani realised that they had pulled up outside the restaurant.

'I have to nip in here and do some errands,' said Kabir solemnly. 'Why don't you two come in?'

Nani was about to say, 'No thank you,' when Salma shivered.

'Yes, let's,' Salma said. 'It will be warmer than staying in the car.'

Nani had no choice. She stepped out on to the wet pavement and pulled her coat even tighter around her.

It was nice and warm inside the restaurant. The plush red velvet chairs were filled with people enjoying the food and the waiters were busy rushing steaming trays to the tables. Kabir walked to the steep stairs that led to the second floor. Nani didn't want to climb the stairs. She was tired. She just wanted this evening to be over so that she could get on the plane tomorrow and go home. But Salma was behind her, practically pushing her up the stairs. With an effort Nani climbed up.

The room at the top was dark. Perhaps there was a power cut. The minute Nani stepped through the door a powerful light snapped on, almost blinding her with its suddenness. Then a chorus of voices burst into a familiar song. Nani stood shocked, a lump formed in the back of her throat and her vision went so watery that she could hardly make out the array of singers, standing beneath an enormous banner, on which had been painted:

HAPPY 75th BIRTHDAY, NANI

Nani reached into her pocket and pulled out a tissue just as the song came to a resounding end. Everybody cheered. People pressed around, congratulating her, so many familiar faces, so many new friends.

'I . . . I . . . don't know what to say.'

Then she caught sight of Jazeera, radiant in a new party dress and grinning cheekily.

'It was you!' Nani cried with realisation. 'You planned all this, didn't you?'

Jazeera hugged her grandmother tightly. 'You never guessed though, did you?'

'You little rascal.'

Music struck up from the band of musicians at the far end of the room and the strains of a melodious *ghazal* wound through the air. People became infected with the party spirit and soon the room was filled with laughter, music, eating and present-opening.

Nani sat like a queen in her court as people came up to her, kissed her and gave her their presents. Soon she was surrounded by a mountain of shredded wrapping paper, curling ribbons and a teetering pile of gifts.

When the present-opening had

subsided Jazeera brought out one last small parcel wrapped in shiny gold paper.

'This one is from me, Nani,' she whispered.

Nani peeled off the paper to reveal a solid silver photo frame surrounding a smiling picture of Jazeera's Nana.

Nani's fingers traced gently over the intricate pattern on the frame and tears pricked at the back of her eyeballs.

'This is perfect.'

Nani leant forward and kissed Jazeera's nose.

'You are too good to me. There, look, I'm going to start crying again.'

Jazeera smiled, she knew her grandmother very well.

Nani sat contentedly with Jazeera by her side, watching the guests enjoying themselves, eating good food and dancing to the music. She had talked to everybody and they all said how much they would miss her. Nani was so happy that she didn't know whether to laugh or cry. No one had ever given her such a big party before. She would remember this holiday for the rest of her life.

Words that you may not know:

Apa	term of respect for an older sister or female relative
Beyti	term of affection for a young girl
Bhangra	type of music
Dhobi-wallah	laundry man
Ghazal	song
Mendhi	Intricate patttern painted on a bride's for decoration
Parathas	stuffed and lightly fried flat bread
Salwar kameeze	trouser suit

Adèle Geras

MY GRANDMOTHER'S STORIES

A visit to her grandmother is an event always looked forward to by the girl at the centre of this book. Her grandmother tells her stories from the long tradition of Jewish storytelling, stories of fools and wise men, of domestic dilemmas and faraway places.

Included in the Children's Book Foundation's 100 Best Books for Children 1991 selection, *My Grandmother's Stories* also won the Sydney Taylor Award of the Association of Jewish Libraries in the United States.

"wonderfully vivid . . ."
>   *Children's Book Foundation*

"a delightful book . . . a volume for any age to treasure."
>   *Junior Bookshelf*

Julia Jarman

THE JESSAME STORIES

Jessame (sometimes called Messy Jessy – when she's messy – or Baddy Addy when she's naughty) is a lively, imaginative, loving little girl to whom exciting things happen.

Jessame has lots of adventures with the magical Grandpa Williams, Uncle Sharp who goes to sea and brings her back unusual presents from faraway places, and fun-loving Aunt Gbee who comes to stay from Africa.

"warm, humorous . . . written with rare understanding . . ."
Sunday Telegraph

"thoughtful, reader-friendly adventures . . . pure joy."
Gloucestershire Echo

Geraldine Kaye

BIRTHDAYS IN SMALL STREET

Happy Birthday to Poppy's pigeon and Poppy's baby brother and Susie and Ben! There are lots of birthdays in Small Street. There are other excitements, too, when Tong goes to London to celebrate the Chinese New Year and Leroy decides to make the Big Fierce Dinner Lady like him.

The third collection of stories about Small Street, where all the houses are the same and all the people are different. The first two books, *Summer in Small Street* and *Winter in Small Street* are also available from Mammoth.